"Ketchum Kids"
Grace + Luke

Merry Christmas
⭐
2010

Love You!

Grandma +
Grandpa Tom

A PHOTOGRAPHIC FANTASY

First Snow
in the Woods

Carl R. Sams II & Jean Stoick

Acknowledgements

We would like to thank our loyal staff: Karen McDiarmid, Becky Ferguson, Ryan Ferguson,
Bruce Montagne, Tom and Margaret Parmenter, Mark and Deb Halsey,
Nancy Higgins and Kirt Manecke
for their contributions in the creation of this book;
Carol Henson (The Book Doctor) for her editing;
Laura, Rob, and Diane Sams for their creative suggestions;
also thanks to Hugh McDiarmid, Mark and Janelle Larson,
Jennifer, Rachel and Lauren Ferguson for their thoughts and ideas.

Special thanks to Heiner and Diane Hertling for their artistic contributions;
Greg Dunn of Digital Imagery for his color expertise;
Danny, Sue and Nancy Boyd for their support.

Carl R. Sams II Photography, Inc.

361 Whispering Pines
Milford, MI 48380
800/552-1867   248/685-2422   Fax 248/685-1643
www.strangerinthewoods.com
www.carlsams.com

Karen McDiarmid – Art Director

Sams, Carl R.
First Snow in the Woods: A Photographic Fantasy
by Carl R. Sams II & Jean Stoick, Milford, MI
Carl R. Sams II Photography, Inc. © 2007

Summary: A fall tale of changing seasons. The great gray
owl came down from the far north and carried
the message, "Winter is coming early. Prepare!"
Will the animals of the forest be ready?

Printed and bound in Canada
Friesens of Altona, Manitoba

ISBN 978-0-9770108-6-8
Fawn (white-tailed deer) / Nature / Fall-Winter
For children of all ages.

Library of Congress Control Number: 2007905490

10 9 8 7 6 5 4 3 2 1

*For those who protect
wild places and love
wild things.*

The northern lights faded bright to dim,
like a distant torch
        flickering across
the cold,
        night sky.

The owl had seen
        all this before,
but something
        was
                different.

Something
told him
        tonight
        he must begin
        a long journey
                south.

In a morning meadow far away,
fog tiptoed in without a sound.
Dew sparkled on fragile webs
where a family of deer grazed.

A soft breeze crossed the meadow
and whispered,
"Do you know what's happening?"

The spider
spun her web
and tidied up a fly
into another tasty bundle.

In the same meadow,
a woolly bear inched his way
along a fern
then onto another . . .
chew, chew, chewing,
doing what woolly bears do.

A dragonfly
    waited patiently
        for his wings to dry.

He had hatched during
    the mid-summer green . . .
        long, long ago in dragonfly time.

When will the new season begin?

When dragonflies no longer fly.

A noisy chipmunk
broke the silence of the meadow.

"Hey, Spotty!
You don't look so good,"
he called out,
munching a tiny, red crab apple.

"You're losing your spots
and your coat
is looking scruffy.

Better start hiding your acorns!"
he warned.

"Why would I
want to hide acorns?"
wondered the fawn.

"Acorns are everywhere."

As the summer faded,
the sweet nectar plants
no longer flowered.

Soon the monarch would follow
a distant memory.

On fragile wings,
his heartsong would lead him
to a tropical garden
thousands of miles away.

The hummingbird
heard the same green song
playing in his head . . .

a gentle memory
of a far-away place.

The tiny traveler
would leave the meadow
that morning.

It was a time of change.

Dewy webs hung on goldenrod
and covered
the morning fields.

So many
woodland birds
had left for distant places
taking their songs
with them.

At the edge of the woods,
a small squirrel
chattered.

"Have you heard?"
asked the red squirrel.
"The great gray owl
is on his way from the far north.
He only stays here
during the
harshest winters."

The wind ruffled
her fur as she
snatched up
a double acorn
to tuck away.

"The first snow
is coming . . .
it's coming early!"

A woodchuck squeezed
out of his hole
blinking his eyes.

"I'm only going to say this one time,"
announced
the old grump.

"Hibernate!

Hibernate!

HI-BER-NATE!"

The sun melted the frost from the meadow,
pushing away the fog
and warming the shadows.

"Are you listening?"
asked Mother Doe
standing quietly.

"It's happening."

The frost had silenced
the wings of the dragonflies.

"The new season
is here,"
she bleated softly.

Leaf by leaf
the green world
gave way
to blazing reds
and golds.

The painted turtle
    climbed onto a rock
        warming himself
      in the fading rays of the sun.

    "Soon I will bury myself
        into the thick mud
      and sleep until spring.

It's what turtles do."

A red maple leaf held stubbornly,
twisting and turning
on its stem.

"Let it happen,"
nudged the breeze.

And so it did,
breaking away soundlessly,
floating down . . .
twisting and
turning.

The fawn was
paying attention.

"Why are the leaves falling?
Why is my coat changing?
Where have so many
of the birds gone?"
asked the fawn.

"All things change."
Mother Doe spoke in
a gentle voice.

"All creatures
must prepare
and be ready to follow
their heartsong."

The fawn didn't feel ready.
Did he even have
a heartsong?

Yet, as the evening
slowly darkened the woods,
he felt safe with his mother
at his side.

Each night stole
more light from the day
and held back
the morning sun.

Honking geese
flew across the sky
announcing the
changing season.

The raccoon poked his head
out of a snug hole in a tree
to listen to morning sounds
and sniff the cool air.

He'd hunted frogs and crayfish
in the moonlight along
the muddy pond.

At daybreak he overturned
rotted bark, finding plump grubs
and runaway beetles.

His heartsong played softly
in his head.

"Can you feel it?
It's coming."

"Good morning!"
"Good morning!"
said the two mice,
peeking out from under the leaves.

"Today is the day!"
"Today is the day!"
they both agreed.

"Today is the day?"
questioned the fawn
with frosted breath.
" I . . . I don't understand."

"It's true!
It's true!
I've heard it too!
The great gray owl is on his way
down from the far north,"
called out the chickadee-dee-dee.

"Are you ready-dee-dee?"

"Ready?
Ready for what?"
questioned the fawn
as Mother Doe
just kept munching
her acorns.

The snowshoe hare
    balanced a white paw on a small tree
as she chewed its tender needles.

        Soon her fur
            would be totally white.

        In winter,
            white is good.

                    Suddenly,
                        a dark shadow
                        soared above
                            the rabbit's head.

The great gray owl
landed with
ruffled feathers on the top
of a swaying spruce.

He had ridden
the north winds many miles
with a storm
on his tail.

"Creatures of the forest!
Prepare!
The first winter storm
is here!"

"But . . . I'm not ready,"
said the fawn
standing all alone.

The snowflakes
floated downward
covering the
meadow.

"What is happening?
Why can't everything
stay the same?"

The wind turned
colder
and the snow
fell harder.

The fawn shook
the wet snow
from his ears.

"I don't like this."

The robin
  agreed.

He wished he had
left earlier,
leaving
his sweet berries
behind.

"Hey!
Where is your home?"
called out a frantic chipmunk.

"Don't you know
you need a hole?
Here!
I'll help you dig.
I'll make it big!"

"A hole in the ground?"
wondered the fawn.
He shook his head.

"But where is my home?
Where should I go?
I'm not ready."

"You *are* ready."
Mother Doe spoke softly
as she appeared
out of the storm.

"You *are* ready
for the first snow
of the season.
Come . . .
follow me.
We will travel
with the rest of our family
to the cedar swamp.

There we'll find food and shelter
and escape the
winter winds."

The owl watched
from above
as the small family of deer
made their way
down . . .

down . . .

down to the low ground
where the cedar trees
grow thick.

Whistling winds
and white snow
swirled and whirled
all through the night

and then . . .

silence.

The fawn woke up
with deep snow all around him.
The whiteness
made him blink.

"Nicely done!
You *are* prepared!
You're almost as plump as me,"
said the fox squirrel.
"And that thick winter coat
will keep you
warm and dry."

As the fawn looked about,
he heard the familiar calls
of the winter birds . . .
chickadees,
cardinals
and blue jays.

A calm came over him
as he listened
to the snow
falling softly.

Now, he knew he was ready.

He had found his winter home.

He *had* heard
his heartsong.

THE END